THE

LIGHTED WAY

~ or ~

Loving Words About Jesus

By COUSIN BESSIE

Grace & Truth Books
Sand Springs, Oklahoma

THE LIGHTED WAY

ISBN # 1-58339-103-7

First published by The American Baptist Publication Society
Previously printed by Triangle Press, 1996
Current printing, Grace & Truth Books, 2005

Cover Art by Scott Baldassari
HC 30, Box 64-B
Pelsor, AR 72856
http://www.geocities.com/scottbaldassari/

Cover design by Ben Gundersen

Grace & Truth Books
3406 Summit Boulevard
Sand Springs, Oklahoma   74063
Phone: 918 245 1500

www.graceandtruthbooks.com

TABLE OF CONTENTS

		Page
1. Christ Our Way	. . . .	1
2. Christ Our Redeemer	. . . .	7
3. Christ the Bread of Life	. . . .	17
4. Christ Our Light	. . . .	25
5. Christ Our Shepherd	. . . .	39
6. Christ Our Door	. . . .	45
7. Christ the Fountain of Life	. . . . .	51
8. Christ the True Vine	. . . .	59
9. Christ Our Life	. . . .	65
10. Christ the Friend of Little Children		73

Chapter 1

Christ Our Way

If you were wandering about, in a thick wood, far from home, and not knowing how to find your way back; if you were trying to force your way through briers that wounded you, and there was no path that you could see; if you knew that there were snakes and wild beasts among the thickets; if night was coming on, and you were cold and tired and frightened, how glad you would be to come upon a plain *WAY* which would lead you straight to your father's house. Would you not think it the pleasantest sight you had ever seen? Ah! You can never know how glad such a way would make you, unless you have really been lost and begun to feel as if you would never find your beloved home. I remember when I was about seven years old, finding myself once, with my two little brothers, both younger than I, in a thick wood, a mile away from home, after the sun went down. We were really in no danger, for there was nothing in the woods to hurt us, but sadly afraid of getting out of the road, though it lay straight before us. But it grew dark and we could not see the path. We kept close together, holding each other's hand, and crying bitterly, wishing we had gone home sooner. Very glad indeed we were to hear presently our father's voice, calling to us to take us safely home.

Now, you, my young reader, are in a wilderness. This world is not our home; it is only the country we must pass through in order to get home. Our home, our Father's house, where we are to live with Him forever, is above. It is a beautiful and happy home, where no sorrow, no sickness, no sin ever enters. And there is but one *WAY* by which we can reach it; but one path through this wilderness world, which will lead us safely and surely to our Father's house on high. It is about this way I intend to talk to you; it is in this way I would like to guide you. Christ is this way; He says himself "I am the way," and you know that what the Lord Jesus says must be true.

I told you that you could not know how glad it would make you to see a plain, safe path opening before you, unless you had been lost, and looking for such a road in vain. You would then know the value of it, by having felt the want of it. Unless you feel that you are lost, and wandering in this world far from your Heavenly Father's happy home, you will not care so much about knowing that Christ is "the way". This is what we call a sinner's "awakening" to a sense of his lost and ruined condition. You must feel that you are lost, undone, incapable of ever finding the true way back to God by your own efforts, and that unless Jesus has revealed Himself as the only Way and grants you

2

the grace out of heaven to believe in Him, you are like one who wanders about in a forest, where there is danger, every moment, of perishing. (Scripture reveals that God commences, continues and completes His salvation in a poor lost creature.) Ah! I cannot make you feel or know this; that is the work of the Holy Spirit alone. He must "take of the things of Christ, and show them unto you." But He is pleased to work by human means, and it may be that He will bless these simple words, and use them to show you your condition in the sight of God, and the way to find safety and happiness.

This world is very fair and pleasant, and seems not at all like a wilderness, and if there were no sin here we might be very happy. And so in the woods of which we have been talking, it looked bright enough while the sun shone, and in some places there grew beautiful flowers and sweet berries; it was pleasant to walk through it, or to stay there for a little while, but it was a poor place to spend the night in, or to be caught in by a storm.

So with this world; our Heavenly Creator gives us a great many earthly blessings, but He does not mean that we should make our home here. He means that we should walk steadily and firmly through it, enjoying every comfort that He places in our way, but not setting our hearts on anything but this: to find and to keep the one way by which we may serve and please Him, and at last reach the safe and happy home which Jesus is preparing for all who love Him.

3

Storms often overtake us in this world, making us long for shelter. There is the storm of sorrow; how dark everything looks to us when some dear friend has been taken away by death; even children have to meet this storm sometimes. It may be a little brother or sister whom you fondly loved, or worse still, a tender mother or kind father, who is laid in the silent grave out of your sight; and what a wilderness that makes this world seem like. Oh! I do not know what people do at such a time who have not learned that Christ is the way; who cannot go to Him and find in Him comfort that they need!

Then, there is the dark hour of sickness; and this, too, is one which children feel, as well as older persons. And the storm of temptation, driving them to do what is wrong, and so making them wretched. And many other storms, of which I cannot now speak, making everyone feel, sooner or later, that earth is not a home, and that their great need is a safe and happy home.

And Christ is the refuge of the soul. Just as soon as you are granted the privilege to believe in Him with all your heart, you see in Him a fulness so large, so immense, that will meet all your needs on your journey. The sooner we are stripped of all our own endeavors, the sooner we are brought on the "way that leadeth unto life", that "strait and narrow way" which will take you safe home where there are no more storms, no more sorrow, no more sin. Will you not come to Jesus? Will you not walk in this safe way? It is a pleasant as well as a safe road; "All

4

its paths are peace." Do not wait until you are older; you will find it a great deal easier to come now than if you wait till you have wandered further into strange paths, and got entangled in the long grass, and among the briers of sinful habits. Come now into the right way; learn to love Jesus while your hearts are young and tender. He will forgive all your sins, and lead you safely through all temptations, and all the storms of life. And as you go on in this blessed way, you will find it become plainer and easier. The more you strive to serve Jesus, the more you will love Him, and the happier you will be. And the nearer you come to the end of your life's journey, whether it be long or short, the brighter will the light fall upon it from the glorious home to which Christ is leading you. When the night of death gathers around you, you will be able to say, "I fear no evil." Christ never forsakes at the last those who have walked with him through life.

Come then and set your little feet in this one, only safe way! To do so, you have only to be sorry for your sins, to confess them and to pray to God earnestly if He will grant you the faith out of heaven to believe in the Lord Jesus Christ with all your hearts, and to try, by the help of the Holy Spirit, always given to those who ask it, to serve and to please God.

Come, children, come to Christ today,
He is the safe, the heavenly way,
The way to God, the way to heaven,
The way to have your sins forgiven.

Come little ones, to Jesus come;
Jesus will lead you safely home;
He died for sinners; do not delay
To seek His love. He is the way,

The only way: no other road
Will lead us, sinners, home to God.
Come, little children, do not stray
In sin, but come to Christ today.

Chapter 2

Christ Our Redeemer

Do you know what a Redeemer is? It is one who helps another out of any trouble, or difficulty, or punishment, by bearing it for him, or paying the penalty in his stead.

Some little children once had a pet lamb. They had taken care of it since it was very small; it ran after them, and ate from their hands. They loved it almost as much as they did each other. But one morning when their lessons were done, and they ran as usual to play with "Snowy" as they called it,—it was so white, —the lamb was nowhere to be found. They ran all over the garden, calling it, and then out into the lanes and fields nearest their house, but no Snowy could they find, and they came back sorrowfully to tell their mother. She was sorry, too, that they should lose their pet, and went with them to look at the little meadow where they kept it. Everything was just as they had left it the evening before, when they went to bid Snowy good night, and they came to the conclusion that someone must have stolen their lamb; that it would run away was not to be thought of; it loved its home and its

And running forward, they reached the corner of the road just as a large, rough-looking boy came along, dragging a little white lamb by a rope around its neck.

playmates too well for that. Their father was away from home, or he would have tried to find it for them, so after dinner, which they could hardly eat for talking about their loss, the children asked their mother if they might not go into the town, nearly two miles off, and look for their lamb. After some hesitation, she consented, making them promise that they would take care to be at home before dark.

So off they started, in hope of finding their pet; all the way they were calling, "Snowy! Snowy!" and running to look behind every hillock that they passed, but they saw nothing of it until they had almost reached the town. Then, as they were hurrying along, they heard, down a cross-road which they had almost reached, the bleating of a lamb. "Oh! that's Snowy!" they all cried, eagerly, "there she is now!" and running forward, they reached the corner of the road just as a large, rough-looking boy came along, dragging a little, white lamb by a rope around its neck.

"What are you going to do with Snowy?" exclaimed the children, running up to him, "That's our lamb," and poor Snowy, glad enough to see her old friends, tried hard to get away from the boy, and ran to meet them, bleating all the while as loud as she could. "Your lamb indeed!" said the boy as they all gathered round him, "That's very likely." "It is our lamb," exclaimed Ralph, the eldest of the little group, "you see it is; just look how she is licking

Adie's hands! Some wicked person stole her from us last night, and we have come out to find her."

"It won't do you much good now you have found her, I reckon," said the boy. "My master bought her this morning, and she is so nice and fat that I am taking her to the slaughterhouse now."

"To the slaughterhouse! Kill our Snowy! You shall not do it!' cried Ralph, with crimson cheeks and sparkling eyes, while the other children broke out into loud exclamations, putting their arms around Snowy, and one of the boys trying to snatch the rope out of the butcher's hand.

But he held it fast and told them to get out of the way, but they could not do this. They could not let Snowy, their own little Snowy, go to be killed, so there was a terrible time, the butcher pulling at the rope and threatening to strike them if they did not let the lamb go, the children crying, and poor Snowy bleating with all her might.

There is no doubt as to how it would have ended, for the boy was a great deal stronger than they, but just then a gentleman rode up on horseback, and asked what all that noise was about.

"It is our lamb, sir!" said Ralph, half choked with trying not to cry; "It was stolen from us last night, and he's going to kill it." The butcher explained that it had been sold to his master, and that he must do as his master ordered him.

"Oh! nonsense!" said the gentleman, "there, there, children, stop crying! The lamb shall not be killed this time! Give them the rope, Bill. I'll pay your master what he gave for the lamb. Ah, here he comes!"

And, sure enough, the butcher, attracted by the noise, was coming to see what was the matter. He did not like giving up the lamb at all at first, but the gentleman insisted upon his doing so, and, paying him out of his own purse, told the children to take their lamb home, and not let it get stolen again.

How glad those children were then, how they hugged poor Snowy, who had been in so much danger, and thanked the gentleman for his kindness. Now this was *REDEMPTION:* poor Snowy could not save herself, and the children, dearly as they loved her, could not save her, for they had not money enough to pay the price. But the gentleman paid the money, and redeemed the little lamb from death, and the children from sorrow of losing her.

My child, you, too, are lost and in danger of perishing eternally if you do not love Jesus, as much as this little lamb was in danger of being killed, and if Jesus had not pitied us and redeemed us, we must all have perished. The Apostle says we were "sold under sin," as this lamb had been sold to the butcher by the wicked man who stole it, but Christ had compassion on us, and paid the price of our redemption, not with silver or gold, but with his own precious blood.

There is another way of redemption about which I want to tell you a little story, too. It is to rescue another from punishment or suffering by taking it ourselves in their stead, as the little boy did, of whom I am going to tell you.

There were two little twin brothers, Walter and Willie; they were just the same size, and looked so much alike that hardly anyone could tell by looking at them which was Walter and which was Willie. But they were not so much alike in behavior, for while Walter was almost always good and obedient, Willie was full of mischief, and often forgot to do what he was told. One day their mother promised them that in the afternoon, if they were very good, she would take them to their uncle's, a few miles off, to spend a day or two with their little cousins. They were greatly pleased to hear this, for they loved to ride in their uncle's wagon, and to play with old Towzer, his great, good-natured dog, and they talked all the morning about what a fine time they would have.

Soon after dinner their mother dressed them very neatly, and told them to sit down quietly at the front door, or play about on the porch, until they saw their uncle drive up in his wagon. "And mind," said she, "do not go off into the grass or the mud to play, and soil your clothes, for I have no more clean ones to put on you, and if you tear or soil these, I shall have to leave you at home.

The boys promised to be very careful, and they sat down in the front porch very quietly for a while. They had some nice little books and pictures to play with, and blocks to build a house.

But Willie soon grew tired. "Come, Walter," he said, "let's go play down in the garden; I don't want to stay here all the time till uncle comes."

"Oh no," said Walter, "mother told us to stay on the porch, and uncle will be here directly." "He won't come yet," said Willie, "and I mean to just run down and see if some plums have not dropped from the tree."

Walter tried to persuade him not to go, but away he ran. He meant to be very careful to keep his clothes clean, but in hunting for the plums among the green grass, he forgot that. Then, his little dog, seeing him there, came running after him to have a romp, and as Rover had not been at all particular to avoid the mud puddles, his fore-feet left their mark upon Willie's white apron.

But Willie never noticed it, and he got so busy playing that his mother had called him two or three times before he heard her. When he did, and came running up, thinking only that his uncle had come, he was rather a sorry sight. His nice apron and his clean trousers were all marked, too, with mud from the dog's paws. "Oh! Willie! Willie!" said his mother, "What am I to do with such a disobedient little boy? Did I not tell you to stay upon the porch and keep yourself clean? And now look at you! You will have to go up to your room, and stay there; you are not fit to go to your uncle's."

At this Willie began to cry and to beg his mother to let him go, but she only replied, "How can I, Willie? Even if you did not deserve punishment, as you do, for your disobedience, I told you I had no more clean clothes. You would not surely like to go to your uncle's in that dirty condition."

Willie cried as if his heart would break, but that did not help the matter at all, and he was going off to his room in great distress when Walter came up to his mother and said, "Mother, let me change clothes with Willie so he can go to uncle's with you, and I will stay at home."

"Why, Walter!" said his mother, "Don't you want to go to your uncle's?"

"Yes, mother," said he, "but I am so sorry for Willie. Please let me give him my clothes, and stay at home."

"But how would Willie be punished then for his disobedience?" said the mother. "He does not deserve to go."

"I will take his punishment, mother!" said Walter bravely, though the tears stood in his eyes. "Then Willie will be good next time."

His mother did not refuse him any longer, and so Walter's clean clothes were put upon Willie, and he rode away in his uncle's wagon to enjoy a pleasant visit, while Walter, putting on Willie's clothes, stayed at home and bore his punishment for him. He redeemed Willie from punishment by taking it himself.

Now, dear child, our kind and gracious Saviour has taken our punishment for us, dying in our place, that we might live forever. He who had kept the law of God perfectly, bore the punishment which we had deserved for breaking it, clothing us in the clean and spotless robes of His own righteousness, that we might be pardoned and accepted for His sake, and made fit for entrance into His Father's holy and happy kingdom.

This is why we call Him our *REDEEMER,* because He had bought us with His own blood, and saved us from death by dying for us. "Christ hath redeemed us from the curse of the law, being made a curse for us." Oh! Will you not accept the salvation which He has purchased for you at such a price? Will you care more for play, dress, companions,—for every thing and anything almost, than for your merciful Redeemer? Or will you now, in your youth, give yourself to Him who has said, "I love those who love me, and they that seek me early, shall find me"?

God help you to resolve now in His strength, that you will be His disciple, and that, being "bought with a price," you will glorify God in your body and spirit, which are His.

Christ hath redeemed sinners!
He their place hath taken,
And borne the guilt and anguish in their stead;
For them He hung upon the cross, forsaken,
The wrath they had deserved, upon His head.

Christ hath redeemed sinners!
With His own life paying
The price for theirs, He ransoms them from death;
The blessings of His grace to them conveying,
And endless life, by His expiring breath.

Christ hath redeemed sinners!
Even children seeking
To know His love, He will not turn away.
Listen, dear little ones, for He is speaking!
"Will ye not come to me, and come today?"

Chapter 3

Christ the Bread of Life

It must be terrible to be hungry and have nothing to eat; to feel as if one would give anything in the world for even a piece of bread, and not to be able to get it. It makes one's heart sick to think of little children crying for food, and dying for want of it, as they did in Ireland in those terrible famines. We know nothing of such dreadful times in this happy country, for God has always given us food enough and to spare. Oh! how good He is to us! I am afraid we are not half grateful enough to Him for His kindness to us, "filling our hearts with food and gladness." We are so used to having Him take care of us and give us all we want, that we almost forget that everything we have comes to us from our gracious heavenly Father, through Jesus Christ our Lord.

Yes, dear child, "every good gift and every perfect gift cometh down from the Father of lights," that great God who, though He is so high and lifted up, does not forget even a little child like you, but makes the sun shine, and the rain fall, that the earth may bring forth plentifully all that you need. We hardly remember that our food is given us by God, and that if He were not to give it to us, we should be very hungry, and even starve to death.

Our Saviour taught us to pray, "Give us this day our daily bread," but how often do we say those words lightly, and without thinking what they mean! We feel so sure of getting our food that it does not seem as if it could be necessary to ask for it, yet what should we do if God were no longer to give it to such careless, thankless creatures? How easily He could withhold the refreshing showers, without which the green grass, the ripening grain, and everything on which we depend for food must perish! He did so once to punish His rebellious people Israel, "and it rained not on the earth for the space of three years and six months," and "the famine was very sore in the land."

Ah! we cannot realize what it would be to have no food, no bread to eat. I trust we never may! Let us be very grateful to our heavenly Benefactor for the many blessings He bestows upon us, and, from our very souls, say in the words of that beautiful hymn of Dr. Watts,

Are these thy mercies, day by day,
To me above the rest?
Then let me love thee more than they,
And try to serve thee best.

I could hardly find it in my heart to wish, my young reader, that you should suffer from hunger, even for a little while, in order to make you more grateful for your temporal mercies, but there is a hunger which I do earnestly desire that you should feel, for upon it, and upon those who experience it, the Lord Jesus has pronounced a blessing. "Blessed are they," said He to His disciples, "who do hunger and thirst after righteousness, for they shall be filled."

Would that I could make you feel this hunger, for then you would be willing and anxious to come to Christ, who is the *BREAD OF LIFE,* which alone can satisfy the hungry soul. When you run in from school at noon and find a nice dinner on the table, you do not need to be persuaded and coaxed to eat.

Dear child, if you have not come to Jesus and given yourself to Him, your poor soul is famishing, a great deal more hungry than the body which you feed so eagerly. But this is a hunger you never think of, which you do not feel, and so never try to satisfy. May the Holy Spirit help me to find words which will make you conscious of that hunger!

Jesus is good to the hungry soul. He satisfies all its need. David had felt that when he sung, "Oh! taste and see that the Lord is good! blessed is the man that trusteth in Him." If you only knew this, and felt that your soul was starving, how quickly you would try to find Jesus! Instead of being obliged to persuade you to come to Him, to think about Him, and to pray to Him, your parents and teachers, and those who love you best, would only have to direct your eager steps into the right way, and to show you how you could find Him. When I was quite a little girl, I was left to take care of my baby brother for an afternoon. He was beginning to run about a little, but he could not talk. I played with him and amused him very well for a time, but by and by he began to fret and cry, and nothing I could think of would quiet him. I don't know how long I had been showing him one plaything after another, and he pushing them all away and trying to make me understand that he wanted something else, when a little girl, a child of one of the neighbors, came in. She was eating a piece of bread which she held in her hand, and as soon as my little brother saw her he toddled across the room, and, in his baby way, eagerly asked for a share of the bread.

Then I knew what had made him fret so. Poor little fellow! He was hungry, and he could not tell me.

Dear reader! If you were only half so hungry for the Bread of Life, that Bread which came down from heaven, of which, if we eat, we shall never hunger anymore, how eagerly you would seek for it! How gladly you would come to Jesus! This world cannot satisfy your immortal spirit; even now, while you are a child, I do not doubt that you feel that. There are times when you are tired of play, tired of books, tired of everything, and want something, you hardly know what; something that would satisfy you, and of which you would not get tired. I know I felt so often when I was a child; it is the hunger of the soul, which Christ alone can satisfy.

He can; He does; He is waiting to satisfy every hungry, seeking soul. He says Himself that He is more ready to give to those who ask of Him than earthly parents are to give good gifts to their children. Think how kindly and how willingly your father and your mother take care of you and give you all you need, and then remember that the Lord Jesus is more ready to bestow His blessing upon you than even they are. He has proved this by giving His own precious life for you, that you, believing on Him, may live forever.

"Blessed are they that hunger and thirst after righteousness, for they shall be filled." That is His own positive promise; and if you desire to be righteous, you hunger after Christ, for He is "the Lord our Righteousness." There is no righteousness, no holiness but in Him. We can do nothing right without His gracious and ready help, and our best works need to have the robe of His perfect righteousness thrown over them.

If you believe and feel this, you will know what it is to hunger after Christ, you will be as anxious to find Him as you are to get food when you are hungry. And when you find Him saying His blessed word, "I am the *Bread of Life;* he that cometh unto me shall never hunger," you will be ready to say with His disciples of old, "Lord evermore give us this bread!" The Lord of life and glory once fasted and hungered for our sakes. You remember that after His baptism in the river Jordan He fasted forty days, and when the tempter came to

Him he found Him faint for want of food. He was hungry! Our dear Redeemer, to whom everything in heaven and earth belonged! Even one piece of bread would have refreshed Him, yet when the evil one tempted Him to turn the stones which lay around Him into bread, He would not do it, choosing rather to obey His Father's will, and work out our redemption for us no matter how much hunger and suffering it cost Him. He could have made the stones into bread; He need not have suffered from hunger, but He chose to do so for our salvation.

Ought we not to be willing to do anything for such a merciful and loving Saviour? And when all that He asks of us, and that unconditionally, is to believe in Him and to reverence Him, and that for our sakes, not His? It seems strange that anyone can hesitate a moment. There is no happiness, no comfort, away from Christ; only hunger, and emptiness, and want.

Come to Him, then, don't wander away and try to satisfy yourself with the husks of this world. Jesus will give you everything you need in this world, and when you life here is over He will take you to His own happy home above, where you "shall hunger no more, neither thirst anymore," but where you shall be happy in the presence of the Lord forever, for he that eateth of this bread "shall live forever."

*The Bread of Heaven! The living bread
With which Christ's people all are fed;
This is what little children need,
'Tis this which gives them life indeed.*

*No hungry soul is turned away
The gospel feast is spread today,
Ask God to help you freely take,
And eat, and live for Jesus' sake.*

*Will you not come to Jesus now?
Will you not ask Him show you how
To love Him who His life has given
That we might find the way to Heaven?*

*He died that little children may,
Have all their sins clean washed away;
For all your wants His board is spread,
Oh! Come and taste this LIVING BREAD.*

Chapter 4

Christ Our Light

A little boy was once wandering through a forest. It was night, and no moon was shining, and the trees were so thick and so covered with leaves that even if the stars had been bright he could hardly have seen them. But the sky was black with clouds, and the wind was howling among the branches, and the poor child could scarcely see his hand if he held it up before his face, it was so dark.

It was strange for a little boy, not yet ten years old, to be out in the wild woods alone on such a stormy night, but poor Robbie had neither father nor mother in the wide world. His father had died only a little while before, but his mother he could not remember; he had been only a baby when she was taken from him. But she was a good woman, and loved the Saviour, and when she knew that she must die and leave her poor baby in this wicked world, with no mother to love him or take care of him, she had him brought and laid beside her. Then laying her trembling hands upon the head of the little one who knew nothing of the great loss he was going to meet with, she gave him solemnly to the

Lord, and asked Him to watch over her baby, and keep him from all the evil that is in the world.

"Be more than a mother to him, O gracious Saviour!" she prayed, "Lead him safely through the wilderness of this world, as Thou didst Thine ancient people Israel. Be his light and his salvation, O Lord, be his light." Even while she spoke, the light in her own eyes grew dim, her voice faltered, and her spirit returned to God who gave it.

So she died, and little Robbie was left a motherless, helpless baby. It is sad to have no mother. Scarcely anyone will care for and love and be patient with a little infant as a mother will. But Robbie's father was kind, and took all the care he could of him, and so the little boy grew up, year after year, to be his father's companion and comfort.

They were poor, and his father had to work hard all day, but in the evening he would sit down on the bench before the door in summer, or beside the fire in winter, and take Robbie on his knee and talk to him about his mother, and tell him how she had prayed for him when she was dying. He would tell him, too, about the place from which he had come, away off, miles across the country, and about his old mother, Robbie's grandmother, who was still living there, and whom he promised that he would, some day or other, take his little boy to see.

"When shall we go, father?" the little boy would ask, and the answer always was, "As soon as you are able to walk so far, Robbie. It would cost more money to ride there than we have to spare."

But before Robbie was old enough to take so long a walk, the poor little boy came home one day from a ramble in the fields to find his kind father just being carried into his house by some men, quite dead. He had been thrown from a wagon he was driving, and his head had struck a stone. Now the poor child was indeed alone in the world, and for a while he could do nothing but cry and sob, for his father seemed to be the only friend he had, and he loved him dearly.

But, after the funeral, a kind neighbor took him to her house, and as he sat there in a corner, with his face in his hands, he heard them talk about him, and wonder what was to become of him. One said one thing, and another, but while they were still talking, Robbie surprised them all by lifting up his head and saying very decidedly, "I shall go to my grandmother!"

He had not thought of it before, poor boy! He had thought of nothing but his father, but now, when he heard them say he must be bound out, or go to the poorhouse, he remembered all that his father had told him about his grandmother, how kind she was, and how much she would love him, and he resolved to go to her.

Nothing that could be said would persuade him not to go, so at last the woman who had taken him told him if he thought he could find the way, he should go in the morning, if he would lie down and sleep that night. Robbie was sure that he could find the way, for his father had told him all about it so many times. He thought he knew every hill, every stream, and every wood that lay between him and his grandmother's home. So, comforted for the first time since his father's death by the hope of soon seeing her, he lay down to sleep.

In the morning, as soon as he had had his breakfast, the neighbor tied up his little bundle, gave him some bread and meat and a few pennies, and he started off to take his first journey in life, the journey which he had looked forward so joyously to taking with his father.

He had been traveling for three days, and was very tired, when he saw before him a village which he thought must be the one in which his grandmother lived, and he hurried forward in hope of soon seeing her. But he was sadly disappointed to find, on inquiring, that Townville was still several miles away. The sun was not very far from setting, and as he looked along the road which they told him he must take, and saw that not far beyond the village it seemed to enter a thick wood, his poor little heart failed him, and he felt as if he could not go any further.

But he had spent his last pennies in the morning for a loaf of bread, which, with some berries he had gathered by the way, had been his breakfast and his dinner. He knew he should be hungry enough in the morning, and should have nothing to eat, and then he thought of his grandmother, and the longing to see someone who would speak kindly to him and love him was so strong that, though his feet ached with walking, he started bravely on again, hoping he might get through the wood before it was very dark.

As the sun went down, the wind began to rise, and the clouds to gather, and before he had reached the middle of the wood it was very dark indeed, and he became bewildered and frightened. At last, still trying to push onward, he stumbled against the root of a tree, and fell. He was not much hurt, but his strength and courage were all gone, and instead of trying to get up again, he just laid his head down and cried. "I shall never get to grandmother's," he sobbed, "I can't go any further, it is so dark. I cannot find my way!"

He did not care so much for being tired and hungry if he could only have kept on his journey, but it was so dark he could not tell which way to go. But, while he lay there moaning and wishing it was light, the thought of his mother's dying prayer, of which his father had so often told him, came into his mind, "Be his light and his salvation, O Lord! Be his light." And, though he had never understood just what his mother meant, he felt now as if light was the one thing he most needed, and getting upon his knees, he clasped his hands, and cried out aloud in his great trouble, "Be my light and salvation, O Lord! Be my light!"

He hardly knew what he expected, poor little boy! But he knew what he wanted, and his father had often told him that God would hear and answer prayer. And no doubt God did listen and take care of the poor orphan boy who had no one else to help him, for, after a time, while Robbie was still praying, he saw a light moving along among the trees. It was a good way off at first, but as he watched it, it came nearer, and presently he heard a quick, heavy tread, and then a cheerful whistle. At that, poor Robbie, half afraid to speak before, took courage and called out for help. "Hallo!" said a loud, pleasant voice in reply. "Who's there?"

"I've lost my way," said Robbie pitifully, "and I'm all alone, and so tired."

"I should think you were," said the man, who had turned out of the path he was following when Robbie called, and had got up to where he was. He turned the light of his lantern full upon the pale face and tearful eyes of the little boy and saw that he was indeed tired and in trouble.

"Poor child!" he said compassionately, "How did you come to be here by yourself such a dark night?"

Robbie told his simple story in a few words, and when he had done, his friend said, "Poor child!" again, and dashed a tear from his eye.

"May I go with you sir," asked the little boy timidly, "till I get out of the wood? I can't see at all, it is so dark, and your lantern is such a help."

"Go with me! To be sure you shall! Do you think I would leave you here in the dark? I'll take you up on my back, if you will."

"He turned the light of his lantern full upon the pale face and tearful eyes of the little boy, and saw that he was indeed tired and in trouble."

But Robbie would not think of that, and cheered by his companion's presence and kind words, and especially by the light which enabled him to see where to step, he almost forgot that he was tired, and walked along quite gaily, answering the questions of his new friend, and telling him all about himself.

"Are you going to Townville, sir?" Robbie asked at last.

"Yes, that is where I live!"

"Oh! Do You? Do you know my grandmother?" inquired Robbie, eagerly. The man laughed out as he replied, "I really can't tell, sonny, as I don't know her name yet. But I reckon I do. I know most everybody in Townville. What's your name?" he added, "I have not asked you that yet."

"Robert Gray," replied the little boy.

"Robert Gray?" repeated the man, as if he were surprised.

"Yes, sir!" said Robbie, "that is my name."

"It is my name, too," said the man, laughing again, "but I suppose that is no reason it should not be yours, though it's a little queer. I always supposed I wasn't the only Robert Gray in the world, though I never happened to meet a namesake before. I wonder now," he continued, as if some new idea had suddenly struck him, "If you can be ..." He lifted his lantern again, so that its light shone upon Robbie's face, but the little boy could not see the look of surprise on his, nor how he nodded his head, for he was in the shadow.

He did not finish his sentence, either, but lowering his lantern, took Robbie by the hand, and hurried on at a quicker pace than they had been going before, and for some time, quite silently. By and by he said, "We are almost through the wood now, and that light you see just before us there is in the window of my house. My mother always puts it there when she knows I am coming home by this road."

"It looks very cheerful, sir," said Robbie, "and your lantern has been a great help, too. I could never have got out of the wood tonight without it. Do you think I can find my grandmother tonight?" asked the little boy, who, now that he was almost out of the wood, began to feel anxious about that.

"Yes, said his companion, opening a gate which led up to the house, in whose window the light was still burning; "I shouldn't wonder if you found her in here. We'll go in and see anyhow."

A nice kind looking old woman opened the door as they came up, and before she had time to ask any questions, her son said, "Take that boy in, mother, and see if you know him." Robbie followed her into a comfortable, neat kitchen, but he was so tired, and the light so dazzled his eyes, just coming in out of the dark, that he did not notice how earnestly Mrs. Gray and her son were both looking at him. At last the old lady spoke, with trembling voice, "He is the very image of what your brother John was at his age. Where did you find him, Robert? Who is he?"

"Ask him," said her son. "Here Robert, come and tell my mother all you have been telling me as we came along, and then ask her to help you to find your grandmother.

He placed his mother in a chair by the fire, and Robbie stood beside her while he told her of his father's having died and left him alone, and of his long journey to look for his grandmother.

"My father's name was John Gray," he said, "but my name is Robert, after my grandfather."

"Then you are my own little grandson, my poor John's child," said the old woman, and her tears fell fast upon his cheeks as she put her arms around him and kissed him, and Robbie cried, too, for joy that he had found his dear grandmother of whom his father had so often spoken to him, and for sorrow that his father was not there too.

Robbie's troubles were all over now, for his grandmother and uncle Robert were very kind, and took as much care of him as his father had done. And he never forgot how good God had been to send him the light he prayed for to lead him out of the dark wood by the hand of his own uncle, who had no idea when he answered the call of the poor, lost boy that it was the child of his dear brother he was going to help. Robbie learned, too, as he grew in years, that there is a better light than that which any lamp or candle, or even the sun can give, and that it was for this light that his dying mother had prayed when she said, "O Lord! Be his light!" And he was led to seek and to find that dear Saviour, who is the true *Light* which lighteth every man that cometh into the world. And now my young reader, do you know why I have told you all this about Robbie. Not only that you may see that God hears and answers prayer, though this is a great truth, and an important lesson to learn. Not only that He takes care of the orphan, and of the helpless and leads them in the right way, though this is also true, and a blessed thing to know and believe. But the lesson which I wish most of all to impress upon you is this: the Lord Jesus Christ is the *Light* of the world. If you are not trying to please and follow Him, you are as much in the dark as was poor Robbie in the wood, and in more danger. You need to pray as earnestly as he did for light. You need to cry with all your heart to God to help and save you, to lighten your eyes, lest you sleep the sleep of death.

Instead of that, you are probably as contented and as careless as if you had all the light you could possibly want, and were in perfect safety. Oh! How strange this is. If you were wandering in the dark as Robbie was, and saw a light in the distance, you would not wait to be told to direct your steps toward it, you would seek it eagerly and of your own accord. Why do you not as earnestly and as instantly seek Jesus, the only true light of the benighted and wandering soul?

Do not let it be your condemnation that you "choose darkness rather than light." Light is better than darkness; righteousness is better than sin; to serve and to please Jesus is the only thing worth living for. Choose this pleasant service, and walk in the light here, that you may live with Christ hereafter, where "there is no night, and they need no candle, neither light of the sun, for the Lord God giveth them light, and they shall reign forever and ever;" where "the city hath no need of the sun, neither of the moon to shine in it, for the glory of God doth lighten it, and the Lamb is the light thereof."

In that land a light is shining,
Such as earth has never seen;
There the day knows no declining,
There no dark nights intervene.

There the blessed Saviour reigneth,
Lighting all the holy place,
And no pain or grief remaineth,
Where the children see His face.

Even here their steps He lighteth,
Though the way be dark and long;
Guards from danger that affrighteth,
Making all who love Him strong.

He is light! To Him be glory!
Little children, join the strain,
Here, and in the world before ye,
Glory to His holy name!

Chapter 5

Christ Our Shepherd

"I am the good Shepherd," said our Lord, "and know my sheep and am known of mine." If you were a Jewish child, living as the Jews did then, in their own beautiful land, you would know all about the care which shepherds take of their sheep. You would know how constantly they watched their flocks, by night as well as by day, feeding them, leading them from place to place, taking care of them, and calling them all by their names. We have no such sight in this country as that of a flock following its shepherd up and down wherever he chooses to go, through green fields and by clear waters. We are accustomed to see them turned into a field, to graze by themselves, without special care or notice being taken of them.

Those who live in eastern countries, or who have traveled there, find it easy to understand what our Saviour means when He calls Himself the *GOOD SHEPHERD*. Though we have never seen, and perhaps never may see, those distant fields where the shepherd knows each one of his sheep, and is known of them, and among which our Saviour walked while dwelling upon the earth, yet we can learn what He meant when He called Himself our "Shepherd." When we read of the shepherd gently leading his flock, and carrying the lambs in his bosom, it is very pleasant to think that our blessed Lord has promised to take the same care of us, and to help us in every difficulty. Do you remember that sweet Psalm of David's in which he says, "The Lord is my Shepherd; I shall not want. He maketh me to lie down in green pastures; He leadeth me beside the still waters. He restoreth my soul; He leadeth me in the paths of righteousness for His name's sake."

David had been a shepherd in his youth, and knew all about the care of flocks. Once, when he was watching his sheep among the hills of Judea, there came a lion, and at another time a bear, and carried off some of his flock, and David, like a good shepherd, went after the wild beast, and taking the lamb away, he killed them both. Doubtless they wounded him while he fought with them for his lamb, but he did not care for that, though he was but a lad, if he could save the flock committed to his care. Ah! David knew all about what he meant when he sang, "The Lord is my shepherd."

And you, my dear child, may know it too, when God the Holy Spirit, through His uncovering work might reveal His Son to you as your shepherd, and the necessity of becoming a lamb of His fold. Listen to these sweet words of our loving Saviour: "I am the good Shepherd; the good Shepherd giveth His life for the sheep." "As the Father knoweth me, even so know I the Father, and *I lay down my life for the sheep.*"

Do you believe on Him? If you do believe on Him and love Him with all your heart, you are His own lamb, the sheep of His pasture, and of such as you He says, "My sheep hear my voice, and I know them, and they follow me; and I give unto them eternal life, and they shall never perish, neither shall any man pluck them out of my hand."

Are not these sweet words? Who would stay away from such a kind and gentle Saviour? If you were really a lamb, do you think you would choose to wander about and have no one to take care of you, and sometimes not half enough to eat, or, if you found a nice pasture, see a lion coming just as you began to enjoy the fresh grass, and have to run away as fast as you could and leave it all behind you, and be afraid to stop running till you were tired enough to drop? Or, would you rather have a good shepherd to lead you out every morning to safe pastures, where you could skip about and feed at your ease, knowing that he was watching all the time that nothing should hurt you, and that when night came he would secure you in a sheltered fold, and still take care of you? It would be a very foolish little lamb, I think, that would not choose to have a shepherd, if it could, and such are we; for by nature we reject the only Shepherd in everything He has to offer. We are foolish indeed! And yet not half so foolish as that child who does not come to the Lord Jesus Christ, and say earnestly and truly,

"I Thy little lamb would be, Jesus!
I would follow Thee;
Samuel was Thy child of old,
Take me too within Thy fold!"

Jesus often, when on earth, spoke of His people as sheep; one of His very last commands was, "Feed my sheep!" And He is just as much our Shepherd now that He sits at the right hand of God, as He was when His disciples could see Him and hear His blessed voice. And there are many respects in which we should all try to be like sheep; you know what gentle and harmless animals they are. In these dispositions we should try to resemble them that we may please our Good Shepherd. The more gentle and loving we are, the more we shall be like Jesus, and the more worthy to be called His sheep.

We should try to be like those eastern sheep of which a missionary tells us, that passing once by a flock, and, having heard it said that they would obey the shepherd's voice, he asked the shepherd to call one of them. He did so, and the sheep whose name was called instantly left its companions and its food, and came to the hand of the shepherd with a prompt obedience he never saw in any other animal.

If we were thus obedient to the voice of our Good Shepherd, how happy we should be! Never wandering from the safe fold and the green pastures which He provides. "He calleth His own sheep by name, and leadeth them out; and when He putteth forth His own sheep, He goeth before them, and the sheep follow Him, for they know His voice. And a stranger will they not follow, but will flee from him, for they know not the voice of strangers." This is another thing in which we should be like them; we should follow nothing which would lead us away from Christ.

If you do not love Christ, if you are not "the sheep of His pasture," how much you are to be pitied! This world is a bleak, cold place, at best, for little lambs who have no shepherd and no sheltered fold. You cannot find any place where you will be safe from that great adversary, the devil, who, like a roaring lion, is always going about, seeking whom he may devour. It is only in Christ's fold that you can be safe and happy. Come to that dear Saviour then, without delay; tell Him that you are a poor, ignorant child, and need His loving care as much as helpless sheep need a shepherd. Ask Him to be *your* Shepherd, and to keep you from all evil and sin in this world, and when life is over here, to take you to His safe and happy fold above.

He will hear your prayer, and will give you all that you need, for He is the Good Shepherd, and He loves His sheep, the purchase of His own blood; He is more ready to hear and to answer than you are to ask. Do you remember the parable which our Lord spoke to His disciples, saying, "The Son of Man is come to save that which was lost. How think ye? If a man have an hundred sheep, and one of them be gone astray, doth he not leave the ninety and nine, and goeth into the mountains, and seeketh that which is gone astray? And if so be that he find it, verily I say unto you, he rejoiceth more of that sheep than of the ninety and nine which went not astray. Even so, it is not the will of your Father which is in heaven, that one of these little ones should perish."

He wants you to come to Him, and let Him take care of you, as the shepherd takes care of the sheep. Will you not come? Will you not say to Him,

Gentle Shepherd of the sheep!
To the shelter of Thy arms,
We, Thy little ones would creep,
To be safe from all alarms.

Thou hast promised Thou wilt be
Our Good Shepherd! Lord, we come,
To devote our lives to Thee,
Never from Thy fold to roam.

Help us! Keep us! May our days
All be spent in serving Thee,
Walking here in all Thy ways,
Till in heaven Thy face we see.

Chapter 6

Christ Our Door

In the midst of a sandy desert in which nothing could grow, and where only wild beasts could live, was built a strong, safe fortress. It had high, thick walls, which no enemy could climb over or break down, and inside of these, tall palm trees lifted their beautiful heads loaded with fruit, and golden oranges and purple figs hung upon smaller trees, and juicy melons lay ripening on the ground.

The castle was built upon what is called an *oasis!* That is one of those spots in the great desert where a spring of sweet, fresh water had made its way through the ground, bubbling and sparkling and dancing in the sunlight. Round it the green grass and plants and trees had sprung up till it looked like a lovely garden, with the dry white sand of the desert stretching all around it as far as the eye could reach. There they had built the castle, and put the strong high walls all around the little green spot to protect it from wild beasts and from savage men who roam over the desert on horseback.

Toward this castle, one day, a weary traveler was trying to hasten. He knew there were enemies behind who sought his life. The hot sun from which there was no tree to shade him, made him faint and sick; he was suffering from thirst, and there was no water. Before him in the distance he could see the old gray castle, and the tops of the palm trees rising above the wall, and he knew there was water, and rest, and safety there. At length he rode up beside the castle walls, but there appeared to be no door through which he could enter; it was all one blank, stone wall. All along it he rode, looking eagerly for some place of admission, the more eagerly because he saw a cloud of dust in the direction from which he had come, and knew that his enemies were following him fast, and that if he could not get inside the wall he would perish, after all the efforts he had made to escape. What would he not have given at that moment for a *door*, an open door, through which he might enter and be safe?

Outside all was danger and distress; inside was safety, refreshment, and rest. And yet if he could find no entrance, he was lost—lost within sight of safety. His enemies were close at hand; in a few minutes more, it would be too late, when suddenly a heavy door, that looked like a portion of the wall itself when shut, was flung open, and then, as he passed through, it swung back into its place and was fastened just as those who sought his life rode up. We are all travelers through a desert, exposed to dangers and enemies of various kinds; to enemies who would gladly kill, not our bodies, but our souls; enemies who try to keep us from entering our Father's safe abode, that "city which hath foundations, whose builder and maker is God." No earthly castle was ever half so secure or so desirable a refuge; in it grows "the tree of life," and "the leaves are for the healing of the nations." Do you not want to enter there, and be safe? Would you not be glad to see a door opened before you, leading into so secure and so blessed a place? The Lord Jesus Christ says to you and to me and to all who are in danger of perishing, "I am the *DOOR;* by Me if any man enter in *he shall be saved,* and shall go in and out, and shall find pasture." Christ is an open door, a door which no man can shut until all his little ones have gone in and are safe.

Do you know what Jesus means when He says "I am the door?" He means just what He does when He says in another place, "No man cometh unto the Father but by me," that it is only through Him and His salvation we can go to God for the forgiveness of our sins, and for the blessing that we need. By His death upon the cross He has opened to us "a new and living way," by which we may, in His name, draw near to God; the only way by which any poor sinful child of Adam can be saved. If you ask how you shall enter in at this door, I tell you, as the Apostle Paul did the jailer at Philippi, "Believe on the Lord Jesus Christ, and thou shalt be saved." "There is none other name under heaven given among men, whereby we must be saved." You must see yourself utterly lost and helpless and sinful, and that God may justly cast you off, and then believe on Jesus as the only Saviour of sinners. You must

47

ask for faith to believe with all your heart that Jesus died to save you from your sins. You must begin to hate sin, and to love Him. You must say in your heart, "Lord, what wilt thou have me do?" And as you begin to realize that you cannot do this in your own strength, pray the more earnestly that God will grant you His irresistible power, enabling you to do what you cannot do yourself.

Why not come to him at once? Do you not want to believe on Him and love Him? Do you not want to serve and to please Him, when you think how kind and good He is? How He bore the agony of Gethsemane, and the insult of wicked men; how He "endured the cross, despising the shame"; how He went down into the cold, dark grave, rising again on the third day, for the justification of His people. What would have become of us if He had not done and suffered all this? Ah! We would have been left at the mercy of our enemies, and perished eternally. The walls of that kingdom where all is pure, and bright, and holy, into which "nothing shall enter that defileth or that maketh a lie," would have been closed against your helpless soul forever, had not Christ, by His precious blood-shedding, opened a door by which all who truly trust in Him may enter and be safe.

There is no safety out of Christ. Our adversary, the devil, like a roaring lion, goeth about seeking whom he may devour. Evil companions tempt us to do wrong, and our own sinful desires and selfish passions will be ever leading us astray.

From all these foes, Christ alone can deliver you;
the only way of safety and escape is through Him,
by faith in His name.

An open door! The way is plain;
Dear Children, come to Jesus!
He'll cleanse our souls from every stain,
From every sin release us.

Oh! Come to Jesus! Trust in Him,
Whose life for sinners was given!
He is the DOOR. Now enter in,
The blessed door of heaven.

Chapter 7

Christ the Fountain of Life

In most of our large cities are to be seen, almost any day in summer, in our public squares, beautiful fountains throwing their silvery spray into the air, and making everything about them cool and pleasant. How we all love to look at them, and listen to the soft music of their falling waters!

There are fountains in the country too, springs of living water, gushing out from the hill-side, or trickling through the meadow. They water the grass and the flowers, and the little birds come to them to be refreshed. Everything that has life needs water. If it is forced to do without it, is sure to die. The good God, our heavenly Father, has provided it abundantly for the need of every living thing. "He sendeth the springs into the valleys, which run among the hills. They give drink to every beast of the field, and the wild asses quench their thirst. By them shall the fowls of the heaven have their habitation, which sing among the branches. He watereth the hills from His chambers; the earth is satisfied with the fruit of His works."

Because water is really one of the most necessary things in the world, the Lord Jesus has chosen it as one of the emblems of Himself. What pure, cold, water is to those who are perishing from thirst, He is to the soul that trusts in Him. He said to the woman of Samaria, "Whosoever drinketh of the water that I shall give him shall never thirst; but the water that I shall give him shall be in him a well of water springing up into everlasting life."

Thirst is very hard to bear. We are told by those who have experienced both, that it is much worse even than hunger. It was the only bodily suffering of which our Lord and Saviour complained when He hung upon the cross, bearing the punishment for our sins. Just before the close of those awful hours of agony, "Jesus, knowing that all things were now accomplished, that the scriptures might be fulfilled, saith, 'I thirst.'" Ah! He, who had revealed Himself by His ancient prophets as the "Fountain of living waters," who had Himself stood in the temple and cried, "If any man thirst, let him come unto me, and drink," He hung there, in the midst of His own creation, suffering from thirst.

It was for His people that He endured all this agony; He thirsted that they might drink of the river of life. He bore their sins in His own body on the tree, pouring out His life-blood; and now, no one who believes on Him need ever thirst. His invitation to all is "Let him that is athirst come, and whoever will, let him take the water of life freely."

There is a thirst of the soul which Jesus alone can allay. If you have ever been very thirsty, and I dare say you have when you have been playing or walking in a hot summer's day, you know something about what this is like. When you came in, heated and thirsty, you did not want anyone to hand you a bowl of sugar, or a plate full of nuts, no matter how well you might like them at another time. The only thing that would satisfy you would be water, and you could not rest until you got it. So when you once feel that you are a sinner, nothing but Christ will content you. Do you know why? Because He alone has power to forgive sins. And when you begin to find out that you have broken God's holy law, and must be punished unless you can find some way of escape, then the only thing that will satisfy you is to find someone who can assure you of pardon.

Jesus can do this, and no one else can, because He has borne the punishment, and satisfied the law, and "is now exalted, a Prince and a Saviour, to grant repentance and remission of sins" to all who believe in Him. This is one way in which He satisfies the thirst of the soul; its thirst, its desire for pardon.

The soul longs for rest and peace. But the world cannot give either, nor can you find it in yourself. There is always something happening that you do not want to have just so; there is always something which you desire that you cannot obtain.

You think perhaps that when you are grown up it will be different; that you will be able then to have things your own way, and to do and to get just what you please. But no! It is never so in this world;

everyone will tell you that. There is always some disappointment or some sorrow that prevents the soul from being entirely happy, and it goes all through life. But the Christian finds this thirst satisfied. Not that Christ's people have their own way and all their wishes gratified any more than other people. You are not to understand that when you give yourself to Jesus—as I do most earnestly plead with you to do—you will never have any more trouble or trial. By no means; the Christian life is one of earnest service and self-denial. Our Saviour tells us we must take up our cross and follow Him if we would be His disciples; and in another place He says, "In the world ye shall have tribulation."

But if you are Christ's disciples, you will know that His will and His way are best, and that He would not let these things happen to you unless it was for your good. And so, though it may be very hard sometimes to bear sickness, and sorrow, and disappointment, yet, when you remember what Christ suffered for your sake, and remember too that He has promised "all things shall work together for good to those who love Him," you are contented to bear what He thinks best. And so He satisfies another thirst of your soul, the thirst for rest.

As God's chosen people were passing through the desert on their way from Egypt to Canaan, they murmured once because they had no water. And the Lord told Moses to take his rod and smite the rock in the presence of the people, and when he did so, God made the water gush out of the solid stone; "the water came out abundantly, and the congregation drank, and their beasts also." So now, out of every hard trial which befalls His people, our good God and merciful Father can make streams of peace and comfort flow, making us happier in our confidence in Him, and our assurance of His love and help, than we could have been if no trouble had happened to us.

The Apostle Paul, in his letter to the Corinthian church, tells us something more about this miracle, which seems even more wonderful. He says, "They drank of the spiritual Rock which followed them, and that Rock was Christ." If this means the water springing from that smitten Rock, which followed them through all their long forty years of wandering in that dry and sandy desert, so that they were never left without it again, how very wonderful it is!* We know it is thus that Christ stays by and sustains those who love Him, in everything that can possibly happen to them in this world. The people of Israel might get very tired of their journey, their feet might ache, and their heads and hearts too, but while this blessed stream was with

---

* *The Jewish tradition, which is by no means improbable, is, that the people made a suitable cart or carriage for this great stone, and drew it with them by oxen in all their subsequent journeyings. A constant miracle in their sight, more impressive than if they traveled always afterward beside a river.*

them, they could never perish from thirst; the living water was always at hand, making it a great deal easier to bear the trials from which they could not escape while in the wilderness. And so Christ gives His children strength and peace in every sorrow and trouble; even in death itself.

And oh! Young reader, after death there will be an awful difference between those who have loved Christ and those who have not.

Remember that terrible picture which our Lord gives us of the lost soul praying for one single drop of water to cool his tongue, and praying in vain! Fearful, fearful thought! To be denied one drop of water, after having through life refused to drink of the living streams freely offered him.

Oh! Do not risk such a terrible doom. Repent of your sins, and believe on the Lord Jesus Christ. Then, whatever else may happen, His presence and His love will be to you like streams of water in a dry and thirsty land, all through this world, and when you die He will take you where you may drink of the "pure river of the water of life, clear as crystal, proceeding out of the throne of God and of the Lamb." "There the Lamb which is in the midst of the throne shall feed you, and shall lead you unto living fountains of water, and God shall wipe away all tears from your eyes."

But there is another purpose for which water is needed; it is for cleansing. How filthy and unfit to be seen our hands and faces and clothes would become if we had no water, and how uncomfortable we should all be! So without the cleansing blood of Jesus, that "Fountain opened for sin and uncleanness," our souls would be even worse off than our bodies without water. The black stain of sin is upon all our souls, but "the blood of Jesus Christ cleanseth from all sin."

How mortified and ashamed you would be if any great man, if your minister, or the President of the United States, were to come to your father's house and find you with soiled hands and clothes. You would not want to stop one minute for him to look at you, but would be off to wash yourself and put on a clean dress as quickly as possible. Now remember that God, who is so much greater than any mortal man, is looking at you all the time, and that He sees your *soul* stained with sin, and clothed only with the filthy rags of your own righteousness. Think how offensive you must be in His sight, who is of purer eyes than to behold iniquity, and fly to the *Fountain* of cleansing which He has provided, in which you may wash and be clean. Put on the spotless robe of Christ's righteousness; He offers it to all who truly repent of their sins and believe on Him. In it, and in it alone, you may stand without fear in the presence of your Heavenly Father. For the sake of what Christ has done and suffered, you will be accepted, and may sit down with Him in white robes, at the marriage supper of the Lamb.

Fount of healing! At whose brink
Even little ones may drink!
Blessed Saviour! By Whose blood
Sinners are brought nigh to God!
We would come to Thee today,
And for pardoning mercy pray!

We are children, yet we know,
When Thou wast on earth below,
Thou didst bid them bring to Thee,
Little children such as we;
We are thirsty,—Jesus! Lord!
Give us drink! Thy help afford!

We are sinful! We would bathe
In the purifying wave!
We would cast our sins on Thee,
Who alone canst set us free!
Even babes Thy power have seen;
Fount of cleansing! Make us clean!

Chapter 8

Christ the True Vine

You have seen a beautiful grapevine, loaded with its purple clusters. Perhaps you have such a vine growing in your father's garden, and know how beautiful it looks every autumn, when its fruit ripens, and how pleasant to the taste its sweet, juicy, berries are!

Did you ever think of it in connection with our dear Redeemer, the Lord Jesus Christ? Everything that we enjoy, everything that is pleasant or beautiful in nature, should make us think of Him and His great goodness, for they are all the work of His hands, and He gives us every blessing that we have. So that we ought all to be able to say,

"In all things fair or bright I see,
Something, oh! Lord, which leads to Thee."

When we have learned to see Christ in everything, and to feel and remember continually that His love is the source from which all blessing flows to us, we shall be happier than we ever were before. It makes every pleasure so much sweeter to think, "The Lord Jesus, who loves me, and who died for me, gives me this; He does not forget me, though He is so far away, and I cannot see Him."

But, though every delicious fruit and every growing plant should remind us of Jesus and His great goodness and love, the *Vine* should especially make us think of Him, because when on this earth, walking about among men and teaching them the way of life, He once said, "I am the true Vine."

Probably our dear Lord was looking, as He spoke, upon one of the many fruitful vineyards of Judea; perhaps He and His disciples had been refreshing themselves with some of the grapes which grew around them. And then, to teach them a lesson they never should forget and to make them think of Him and their relation to Him whenever they should see or eat grapes again, He said to them, "I am the Vine, ye are the branches. As the branch cannot bear fruit, except it abide in the vine, no more can ye, except ye abide in me. If man abide not in me, he is cast forth as a branch and is withered, and men gather them, and cast them into the fire and they are burned." Solemn words! Yet words which even a little child can understand. For you know that if a branch is cut off of the vine, no matter how it may be covered with green leaves, or even with sweet blossoms, it never can bear fruit, but will wither and die. It may not fall to the ground at once; it may be held up by the trellis, but just so soon as it is cut off from the vine, it begins to die, and if it were to stay there forever, it could bear no grapes, nor be anything but a dead useless thing, fit only to be burned. Oh! If you could only understand and feel how necessary it is for you to "abide in Christ," and how, if you do not, you are, like the branch cut off of the vine dead, and without hope. If you could feel this you would lose no time in coming to Christ and in trying to find out what it is to abide in Him.

"Little children," says the Apostle John, the disciple whom Jesus loved, "abide in Him, that, when He shall appear, we may have confidence, and not be ashamed before Him at His coming." Do you ask me how you are to abide in Him? The same beloved disciple will tell you; "He that keepeth His commandments," he says, "dwelleth, (or abideth) in Him, and He in him. And this is His commandment, — the commandment of God, — that we should believe on the name of His Son Jesus Christ, and should love one another, as He gave us commandment."

How kind and loving our Saviour is! If you could only see Him as He is, you would not need to be persuaded to come to Him. I think you could not stay away from Him if you only knew how precious and how good He is. There is no true happiness, no real life, away from the vine, for we get everything that we enjoy from our Divine Redeemer. And in return for all that He gives us He only asks that you will believe in Him and love Him. If indwelling sin and unbelief has the upper hand, ask God to make you a willing servant, enabling you to trust in Him.

If you do this you will abide in Him as the living branches abide in the vine, and He will enable you to bring forth fruit, that is, to live holy and useful lives to His glory and your own everlasting happiness.

Will you not think of these things, whenever you see a grape vine or eat its pleasant fruit! And will you not ask the Lord Jesus, who always hears and answers prayer, to make you a living branch of the true *Vine?* It is by faith in Him, true, earnest, loving belief in what He had done and suffered for you, that you are to be saved from your sins and made one with Him, as the branch is one in and with the vine. Ask Him to give you this faith and love, ask Him to help you to "abide in Him."

Gracious Saviour! Living Vine!
Let us share Thy life divine,
Fruitful branches may we be,
Help us to abide in Thee.

By ourselves we cannot grow,
Of ourselves no fruit can show,
Only as upheld each hour
By Thy goodness and Thy power.

Little children though we be,
Thou hast bid us come to Thee;
Make us branches of the Vine,
And the glory shall be Thine!

Chapter 9

Christ Our Life

"Life! Life! Eternal Life!" cried Christian, when they tried to keep him in the city of Destruction, in that beautiful allegory, which I suppose you have read, called the Pilgrim's Progress.

He had just found out that all who lived in the city where he was born were under sentence of death. So when his friends, who would not believe this, wished to persuade him to stay, he put his fingers in his ears and fled away across the plain, crying out, "Life! Life! Eternal Life!"

By that city of Destruction is meant this world, which "lieth in wickedness," and "is at enmity with God." If children who do not love the Lord Jesus could only see their true state, they too might cry out for "life, eternal life," and run to someone who would show them how to obtain it.

The life of the body is a wonderful and mysterious thing, though it lasts at most but seventy or eighty years. It is the gift of God, to be received with thanksgiving and devoted to His service and His praise. And to most people it is very dear and precious; "all that a man hath will he give for his life." But oh! Of how little account is the life of this poor perishing body, which must soon die and be laid in the ground, compared with the life of the soul, which can never, never, cease to enjoy, or to suffer. It is this life, young reader, that you ought to be thinking of; and should always be trying to secure.

The true life of the soul is in our Lord Jesus Christ. He has purchased it for us with His own blood, freely shed on Calvary. He says to all of us, "I am the Resurrection and the Life; he that believeth in me, though he were dead, yet shall he live, and whosoever liveth and believeth in me shall never die." If He stood among us today, saying to you, as he did once to Martha, in Bethany, "Believest thou this?" Could you reply, from your very heart, as she did, "Yea, Lord! I believe that Thou art the Christ, the Son of God."

Perhaps you would tell me that you believe this. You have been taught from your infancy that the Lord Jesus is the Son of God, the Light and Life of the world, and you think that you believe it; that is, if you think anything about it at all. But have you ever felt that you were lost and ruined without Him? Did you ever realize, like Christian just mentioned, that you had something to do that you might escape from death, and find eternal life? If not, I am afraid you do not know what those words of Christ mean, "He that believeth on me hath everlasting life." Your life is still in danger.

We are totally lost by nature and in danger of hell-fire, yet Jesus is ready, willing, and able to save to the uttermost them that come unto God by Him. He never sends any away without it, who ask Him for it in faith and in sincerity, feeling that there is no life out of Christ, and that unless He saves them from death, they must die forever.

If you were in a dungeon, condemned to be hung for some wicked deed that you had done, and a friend were to come in and tell you that the Governor pitied you very much, and that he said if you were only sorry for what you had done and would promise to try to do right in the future, he would pardon you, do you think that friend would have to persuade and entreat you to see the Governor and ask him to let you go free? I think you would be ready and glad enough to accept the offered mercy, and thank him very humbly for saving you from death.

But, if it were absolutely necessary that someone should be punished for your wickedness, if the law must be satisfied, suppose this good Governor pitied and loved you so much as to bear the punishment himself which you had deserved. How would you feel then? Would it not seem as if nothing you could ever do would be sufficient to show your gratitude and love for such a friend who had given you life at the sacrifice of his own? Yet all this the Lord Jesus has done for you, and how little you think of it, or of Him! How lightly you seem to prize the salvation which He has wrought out for you!

Life! You hardly know all that word means until you have been in danger of losing it, until you know and feel that you are in danger of losing it, for everyone who does not love the Lord Jesus is really every moment in danger of losing the life of the soul.

No, worse than that, we have lost the very breath of life which we received in Paradise. We are spiritually dead in trespasses and sins and never will we see our dreadful condition unless the Lord makes it known to us.

A steamboat was once passing up a broad, beautiful river. It was a lovely day, and the people on board were in high spirits, and enjoying themselves greatly. On the deck some were singing and dancing, and others laughing and talking; nothing was further from their thoughts than death. But all the time, a fire, which had broken out soon after they left the shore, was raging in the hold, and getting sure mastery of the boat. Were they in any less danger because they did not know it? Ah no! In the midst of their mirth and enjoyment, the flames leaped out and came curling and crackling along the very deck on which they were gathered. Did the fact that they did not know or suspect that death was so near alter the reality of their great peril? Surely it would have been a kindness in anyone who knew that they were in such dreadful danger to call out to them, and tell them, and beg them to escape. And I would cry out to you! I would say, "O my child! If you do not belong to Christ, you are in danger of perishing! Come to Jesus! Come quickly, that He may give you life!"

On the boat I am telling you of there was terrible fear and confusion when the people saw their danger. There was screaming, and crying, and praying, and some in their terror jumped overboard and were drowned. The blaze was soon seen from the shore, and here and there a boat put off to come to their help, but there were not enough of them to take in all the people. The pilot who stood at the helm, as soon as he knew that the boat was on fire, turned her bow toward the shore, but the current was against her, and the engine scarcely worked at all, for the flames had soon driven both fireman and engineer from their posts, so that the boat made very little progress; still he kept her headed toward the land, as the only hope of safety. The flames gathered around him, yet he kept his hold upon the tiller, bent upon saving the helpless, frightened passengers, if he could, even at the sacrifice of himself. It was not till the ropes by which he guided the vessel were burned, and he had no longer any power over her, that he would leave his post; then, too much burned and exhausted to save himself, he threw himself, all on fire as he was, into the river, and was drowned; but the boat reached the shore, and many were saved. All were loud in praise of the pilot who had so nobly sacrificed himself rather than abandon the passengers to certain death. Must not those whom he saved have been grateful to him, and have been willing to do a great deal to show their gratitude if he had lived? Oh! I think so! I think if I, or any one dear to me, had been upon that burning ship, and had been saved by the devotion and unselfishness of that brave pilot, I should have felt that nothing I could ever do would be enough to show how grateful I felt.

But the Lord Jesus has done far more than this. He died for poor sinners. He bore such suffering in the garden of Gethsemane and on the cross of Calvary as no mere man, no one but Himself, could have borne. And that to save sinners, not from flames which could consume their body and no more, but from "everlasting burnings," from the "devouring fire," which consumes but does not destroy the soul.

Oh! The death of the soul! The death that never dies! Do not let it be your lot. "Today if ye will hear His voice, harden not your hearts." I know that His commandment is life everlasting; therefore I would speak to you "all the words of this life," and beseech you to plead earnestly for that salvation which the dear Redeemer offers.

The Saviour is calling,
"Say, why will ye die?"
Oh! Come to Him, children, today!
He offers you life; His salvation is nigh;
He bids you no longer delay.

The life that He offers is bought with His own,
He died that His people may live,
And only His blood can for sinners atone,—
He only redemption can give.

Come children, to Jesus! Your Saviour obey!
Come ask Him for pardon and love,
He will guide you through life,
and in death be your stay,
Then take you to mansions above.

Chapter 10

Christ the Friend of Little Children

In this world there is no one who does not need a friend. None are so strong, so rich, or so happy as to be able to do without the love and friendship of others. People sometimes talk of being very independent, and think, or profess to think, they can take care of themselves, as they say, and want nobody to help them. But, sooner or later, there comes a time to everyone in which the kind word and helping hand of a friend is sadly needed and very welcome.

If this is true of grown persons, it must be doubly so of children, who need constantly the loving care of parents and friends. What would become of the helpless infant if it had no one to watch over it and provide for its many wants?

Nor could you, who are old enough to read this book, do better if left entirely to your own care and wisdom. What do you know about buying and making clothing, about preparing and cooking food, or how would you get either without the money which you could not earn for yourselves? For all these, and for many, many other needful things, you are indebted to the watchful tenderness of parents and friends. Without them, you would indeed be utterly helpless and unhappy.

How sweet it is to remember, when we feel our dependence upon earthly friends, who we know may be taken from us by death or may cease to care for us, that there is one in whose friendship we may trust entirely, who loves us and will never forsake us, "a friend that sticketh closer than a brother." The Lord Jesus Christ is this *Friend;* the best friend that any human soul can have; the only friend that never disappoints and never fails the hearts that trust in Him.

Earthly friends are often unable to do for us what we need, and what they would gladly do, if they had the power. If you were sick and in great pain, your parents would gladly relieve you: they would even take the pain themselves if they could in this way give you ease, but they have no power to do so. This is never the case with the Friend of whom we are talking; "All power is given unto Him in heaven and upon earth." There is nothing you need or desire that He *cannot* give you; there is nothing which is really for your good that He *will* not give you, if you ask Him for it in humble faith.

Christ is your best friend. From every other friend we may be separated. And the dearest friends, if they are miles away from each other, can do very little to soothe or help or comfort one another. You might fall off a boat into the river, and the person you love most in the world, if he were far away, would be of no use to you.

The Lord Jesus is never far away. He knows just what we need all the time. He is a Friend always at hand. He has said, "I will never leave thee nor forsake thee." Is not such a Friend worth having, dear little reader? Is He not worth seeking for with all your heart? In the hour of death, when no human friend can go with us into the dark valley, or through the cold river, Jesus is at the side of those who love Him, to help and to deliver them. Death is terrible to those who do not love Christ. Even to Christians it is a solemn hour. How precious at such a time is a friend who can go with you and tell you not to fear, who has himself conquered this last enemy and made the passage to the grave safe and peaceful to all who trust in Him.

You may think that while you are so young, the day of your death is far distant, and you do not need to think about it yet. But children die; almost every day we see little coffins carried to the grave, in which bodies, no larger than your own are laid away to slumber until the resurrection. You do not know how soon the messenger death may come for you. And because you do not know how soon you may be called to die, will you not come to Jesus Christ, the kind and gentle Saviour, and beg Him to love you and to be your friend in life and death, in time and in eternity? Come *NOW*. "Today, if ye will hear His voice, harden not your hearts."

I am sure that if you knew you would die tomorrow you would become very concerned about your condition. However, a concerned soul is not a saved soul as yet, therefore we need Christ to become our friend in life and also in the hour of death. And you are not certain that you will not die, "for what is your life? It is even a vapor, which appeareth for a little time, and then vanisheth away." Jesus is ready and waiting to receive you into the arms of His love, where you will be safe and happy, whether you live or die. He is kind and gentle to all who seek Him, but He is especially the friend of little children. When He was upon the earth, and made in fashion as a man, He showed His love for them more than once, even when His disciples, less gentle than He, would have kept them away from Him. He took them up in His arms, put His hands on them and blessed them. He said, "Suffer little children to come unto me, and forbid them not."

Do you not need just such a *Friend* as Jesus? Can you do without Him? Oh, no! Indeed you cannot. It is because I know that you cannot, that He is the only friend who can make your life or your death happy; that I talk to you so earnestly about coming to Him. You cannot do a great deal for Him who has done so much for you, but you are called to love Him with your whole heart, and try to serve Him in every way that is possible. This is what He asks of you; "Give me thy heart," He says; "take my yoke upon you, and learn of me."

If a king were to tell you that he was your friend, how proud you would be; and if he proved his love and kindness by many costly presents, and told you that you should, after a while, come and live with him in his splendid palace, how delighted you would be, and what wonderful kindness you would think it! You would be always talking about your friend the king, and looking and longing for the time when you should go to live with him.

But Jesus is a king, infinitely greater and mightier than all the kings of the earth put together. Yet he condescends to call Himself your *Friend,* the friend of little children. He has given you more tokens of His love than any earthly monarch could bestow, and has promised that you shall come, if you love Him, to live with Him, by and by, in His glorious palace in the skies, to go no more out forever. Do you love to talk and to think of this friend, of what He has done for His people, and the home to which He is going to take them? Oh! I hope that the Lord will enable you, through His irresistible power, to embrace Jesus as your friend, and spend your whole life in loving and serving Him, so that at the last we may all meet in His heavenly kingdom, and be happy with Him forever and forever.

Friend of little children! Hear us!
All our wants are known to Thee.
Thou of all our friends art dearest;
From our follies set us free.

From Thy throne in heaven descending,
Thou didst tread this earthly ball;
To the least and lowliest bending,
Thou, who art the Lord of all!

Friend of children! Gracious Saviour!
Make us know Thee as Thou art;
With Thy presence and Thy favor,
Fill each little, sinful heart!

Own us Thine! Our souls possessing,
With the fullness of Thy grace.
Onward in Thy ways still pressing,
Till in heaven we see Thy face.